Happy Cat Books

OLD TOM

Written and Illustrated by

Leigh HOBBS

HAPPY CAT BOOKS

Happy Cat Books Ltd.
Bradfield, Essex CO11 2UT, UK

First published by Penguin Books, Australia, 1994

This edition published 2005
1 3 5 7 9 10 8 6 4 2

A CIP catalogue record for this book is available from the British Library

ISBN 1 905117 10 8

Printed in Australia

For Ann James and Jenny Melican

Angela Throgmorton lived alone and liked it that way. One day, while doing some light dusting, she heard a knock at the door.

There, on her front step, was a baby monster.

Angela was curious,
so she carried him in ...

and brought him up.

Angela had never fed a baby before,
and what a strange big baby he was!
She called him 'Old Tom'.

Old Tom grew up very quickly. In fact, it
wasn't long before he outgrew his playpen.

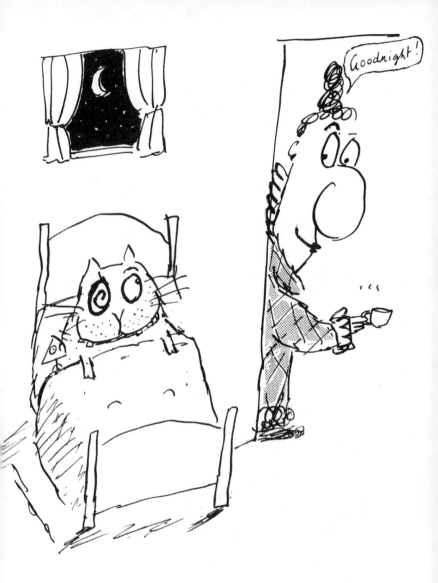

And when he did, Angela gave him the spare room. It was all clean and neat.

Angela taught Old Tom how to behave.
'Sit up straight!' she would say.
'Elbows off the table.'

'Not too much on your fork.'
'Chew with your mouth closed.'

There was so much to learn.

But Old Tom loved bath time most of all,
when he could splash about and make a mess.

He always liked to look his best ...

especially when he went out to play.

At first, Angela ignored Old Tom's childish pranks.

After all, she had things to do and dishes
to wash.

But her heart sank when *someone*
forgot his manners.

Old Tom *tried* to be good ...

though sometimes he was a bit naughty.

'Aren't you a little too old for such things?'
Angela Throgmorton often asked.

As the months went by, Angela tried to keep the house tidy.

It wasn't easy, as Old Tom seemed
to be everywhere.

There was no doubt about it,

he was a master of disguise.

Sometimes Angela heard strange noises
coming from the kitchen,

and whenever she had guests, Old Tom
would drop in unannounced.

Old Tom was out of control.

'When *will* you grow up?' Angela often muttered under her breath.

Sometimes Old Tom went for a little walk
to the letterbox.

But Angela thought it best that he stay inside.
'You mustn't frighten the neighbours,'
she would say.

When babies came to visit ...

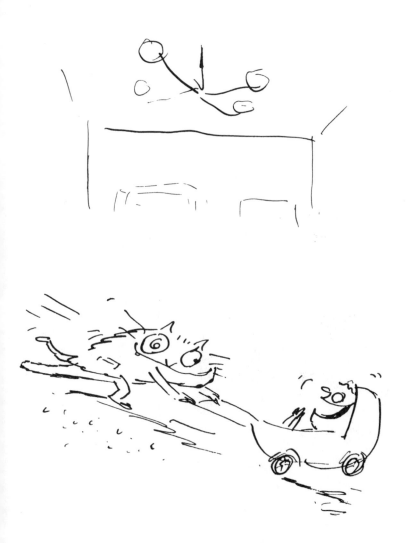

Old Tom loved to play.

'Heavens, what's that in the pram
with my baby!' cried one of Angela's friends
during afternoon tea one day.

It was Old Tom, of course.
Angela was extremely embarrassed.

By now, Angela was having trouble sleeping.

Her nerves were shattered,

CHOO!

and Old Tom's fur had given her
dreadful hayfever.

When she finally did
fall asleep, Old Tom was
often in her dreams.

Angela longed for the good old days,
when her home was in order ...

with everything in its place.

Whenever it was time to help with the dishes, Old Tom felt sick.

He liked to sleep in, and enjoy a late breakfast
on Angela's favourite armchair.

Angela was fed up.

Old Tom had to go.

'At last I have the house to myself!'
cried Angela Throgmorton.

It was a bold move,

but Angela thought it for the best.

Now she was free to scrub ...
and polish,
sweep and mop.

With Old Tom gone, her house would be spick and span once more.

By now Old Tom was in town,

where there were places to see
and people to meet.

In a pet shop nearby, he found new friends to play with.

Some had feathers and one had fins.

But Fluffy the puppy was
Old Tom's favourite.

In the cinema next door the film had
just started.

When Old Tom wandered in ...

he was mistaken for a monster on the screen.

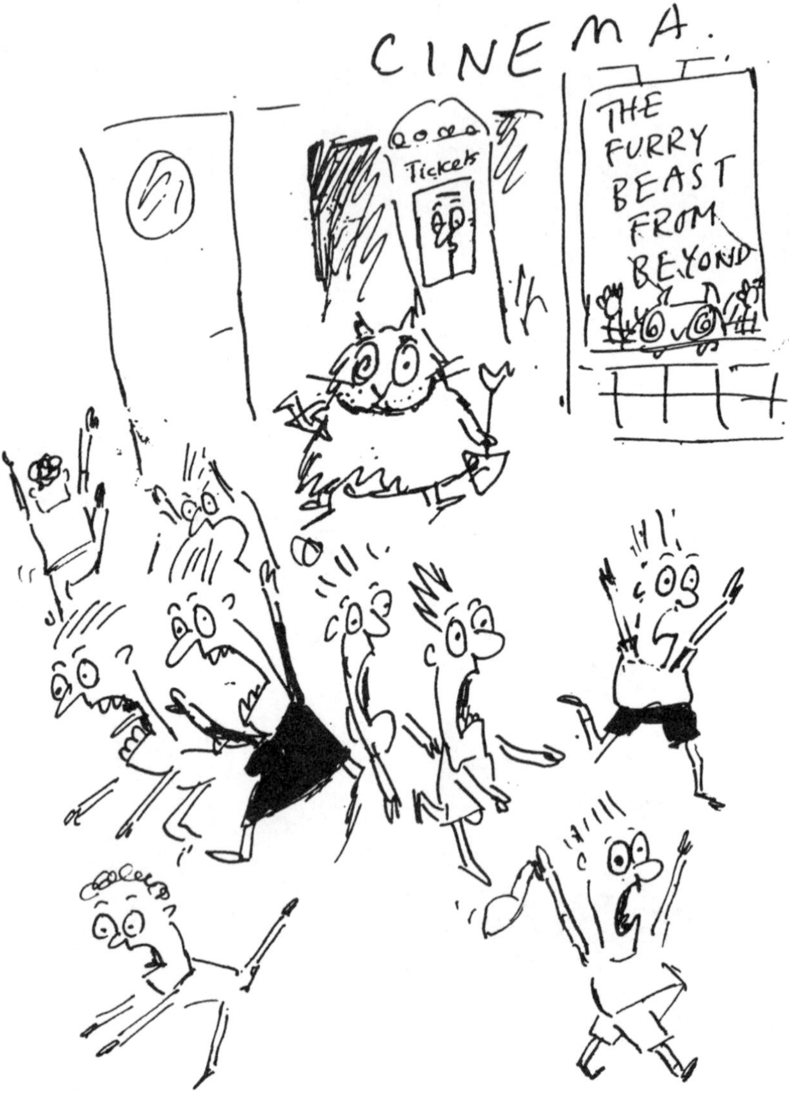
CINEMA.
Tickets
THE FURRY BEAST FROM BEYOND

It was a wonderful surprise when
Old Tom found Happyland.

There were swings and slides,

places to hide,

children to play with ...

and an elephant to ride.

Old Tom was having a lovely time.

But not everyone was happy in Happyland.

When darkness fell, Old Tom was alone.

And when the storm came, he tried to be brave,

even when the thunder boomed.

For Old Tom there was
no breakfast or lunch,

or afternoon tea ...

while far away, Angela was alone in her clean
tidy home.

Old Tom tried and tried to find
someone to play with.

But he couldn't find one friendly face.

There was no fur on her floor, but Angela
still couldn't sleep.

And neither could Old Tom.

He had nowhere to go
and nothing to eat,

until at last he found food at the
bottom of a bin,

where he dreamt of his warm safe bed.

Angela was worried sick.

For poor Old Tom ...

the future looked bleak.

Suddenly there was a news flash

'ORANGE FURRY MONSTER CAUGHT

'That monster is my baby!' cried Angela
Throgmorton.

In no time at all, she was off to the
pound to rescue Old Tom.

'Be quick!' Angela shrieked.

Inside his cage,
Old Tom had just begun to cry,

when suddenly he heard a big voice boom:
'I'm here for my baby!'

Angela was overjoyed.

And so was Old Tom.

AUTHOR PHOTOGRAPH BY PETER GREY

ABOUT LEIGH HOBBS

Leigh Hobbs was born in Melbourne in 1953, but grew up in a country town called Bairnsdale.

Leigh wrote and illustrated *Horrible Harriet*, which was shortlisted for the 2002 Children's Book Council of Australia Book of the Year Awards (Picture Books). As well as *Old Tom*, *Old Tom Goes to the Beach*, *Old Tom Goes to Mars*, and *Old Tom's Guide to Being Good* (Happy Cat Books), Leigh wrote and illustrated in full colour *Old Tom's Holiday* for ABC Books. His latest picture book is *Fiona the Pig*.

Leigh is also a sculptor and painter. He has a passion for English history and London is his favourite city, which he visits as often as possible.

Leigh has two dogs, a Blue Heeler and a Kelpie. He feels no affinity with cats, however, he may well admit to one exception . . .

www.leighhobbs.com

Read these books and join Old Tom
on all his adventures.

 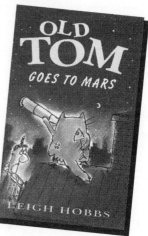

Old Tom at the Beach
Old Tom's Guide to Being Good
Old Tom goes to Mars